J

2016

OCT

THE
GLADIATOR'S
VICTORY

WARRIOR HEROES

Crabtree Publishing Company
www.crabtreebooks.com
1-800-387-7650

616 Welland Ave.
St. Catharines, ON
L2M 5V6

PMB 59051, 350 Fifth Ave.
59th Floor,
New York, NY

Published by Crabtree Publishing Company in 2015.

Author: Benjamin Hulme-Cross

Illustrator: Angelo Rinaldi

Project coordinator: Kelly Spence

Editors: Alex Van Tol, Kathy Middleton

Proofreader: Wendy Scavuzzo

Prepress technician: Tammy McGarr

Print coordinator: Katherine Berti

Copyright © 2015 A & C Black

Text copyright © 2015 Benjamin Hulme-Cross

Illustration copyright © Angelo Rinaldi

Additional illustrations © Shutterstock

First published 2015 by A & C Black, an imprint of Bloomsbury Publishing Plc.

Printed in Canada/022015/IH20141209

Library and Archives Canada Cataloguing in Publication

Hulme-Cross, Benjamin, author
       The gladiator's victory / written by
Benjamin Hulme-Cross
; illustrated by Angelo Rinaldi.

(Warrior heroes)
First published 2014 by A & C Black.
ISBN 978-0-7787-1764-5 (bound).--
ISBN 978-0-7787-1768-3 (pbk.)

       I. Rinaldi, Angelo, illustrator II. Title.

PZ7.H87397Gl 2015   j823'.92
C2014-907828-5

Library of Congress Cataloging-in-Publication Data

CIP available at the Library of Congress

THE
GLADIATOR'S
VICTORY

WARRIOR HEROES

BENJAMIN HULME-CROSS

Illustrated by

Angelo Rinaldi

Crabtree Publishing Company
www.crabtreebooks.com

CONTENTS

INTRODUCTION
THE HALL OF HEROES

The Hall of Heroes is a museum
all about warriors throughout
history. It's full of swords, bows
and arrows, helmets, boats, armor,
shields, spears, axes, and just
about anything else that a warrior
might need. But this isn't just
another museum full of old stuff
in glass cases. It's also haunted
by the ghosts of the warriors whose
belongings are kept there.

Our great-grandfather, Professor
Blade, started the museum. When he
died, his ghost began to haunt the
place, too. He felt guilty about the
trapped ghost warriors and vowed
he would not rest in peace until
all the other ghosts were laid to

rest first. And that's where Arthur and I come in...

On the night of our great-grandfather's funeral, Arthur and I broke into the museum, for old times' sake. We knew it was wrong, but we just couldn't help ourselves. And that's when we discovered something very weird. When one of the ghost warriors touches either one of us, we get transported back to the time and place where that ghost lived and died. And we can't get back until we've fixed whatever it is that keeps the ghost from resting in peace. So Arthur and I go from one mission to the next, recovering lost swords, avenging deaths, saving loved ones, and doing whatever else these ghost warriors need us to do.

Fortunately, while the Professor was alive, I wrote down everything he ever told us about these warriors in a book I call *Warrior Heroes*. So we do have some idea of what we're getting into each time, even if Arthur does still call me "Finn the geek." But we need more than just a book to survive each adventure, because wherever we go, we're surrounded by war and battle and the fiercest fighters who ever lived--as you're about to find out!

CHAPTER 1

"Well, chaps," said the Professor, cheerfully. "What do you know about gladiators?"

Arthur's eyes nearly popped with delight. Even Finn, normally so anxious at the start of a new mission, could not disguise his excitement.

"We who are about to die, salute you!" Arthur chanted, thumping his chest with one hand

and holding the other out in front of him, thumb raised.

"The most highly skilled hand-to-hand warriors of all time," said Finn. "Trained in all sorts of combat styles just to entertain the public in Rome."

"Very good," said the Professor, laughing. "So you do pay attention to some of what I tell you. Mind you, "thumbs up, you live, thumbs down, you die" is probably a myth, and the "we salute you" thing only happened once. But yes, they were specially trained to put on a show and fight in public."

"But I suppose they weren't *real* warriors," Finn mused, as he looked around the Professor's study. He was well familiar with the military items that decorated the walls. "They were part of a public show all about fighting. Just like this museum is, really. It was just a show, wasn't it? Not the real thing."

"Well, yes, it was a sport. But the fighting was real—often to the death, in the early days."

"Of course they were *real* warriors!" Arthur cut in. "What about Spartacus? Wasn't he a gladiator?"

Finn looked at his brother, amazed that he knew who Spartacus was.

"What?" said Arthur, noticing his brother's shocked expression. "I do know *some* things, you know."

Ignoring the boys' squabbling, the Professor went on, "Spartacus certainly was a real warrior. He led a whole army of escaped gladiators in an attack on Rome itself—and very nearly won!

Of course, what he was escaping from was slavery. All the gladiators were slaves. They were owned and traded. They were just treated better than other slaves because they were so valuable."

"But weren't they heroes, too?" Finn asked. "I thought they were celebrities, like athletes today."

"Quite a lot like athletes, actually," agreed the Professor. They had short careers, earned huge sums of money, and had crowds chanting their names from the stands of the amphitheater, while they slugged it out in the arena. They were still slaves, though, and Spartacus realized that an army of highly trained soldier-slaves who wanted to be free would be a formidable force. They were eventually defeated," the Professor sighed. "And most of them were crucified to set an example to other slaves. But they went down fighting as heroes, all at the same time. The fact we all know the name Spartacus two thousand years later is proof enough!"

"And is that how our next warrior died?" Finn wondered out loud. A worried expression spread across his face as he realized he and Arthur would soon be thrown into their next mission.

"Not at all. I don't know why he is not at rest. We think he was quite a celebrated gladiator, actually," said the Professor. "He died peacefully as far as we can tell, probably years after earning his freedom. But we'll find out soon—any minute now, by the look of it."

Sure enough, the atmosphere in the study had changed, just as it always did when one of the ghosts was about to enter. The lights flickered and the clock stopped ticking. The temperature dropped, and all sound and motion ceased.

Arthur and Finn glanced at each other nervously, unsure what was about to enter the Professor's study, and dreading the worst. The door creaked slowly open, and a dark shadow appeared. The warrior who strode in looked every bit the perfect fighter—a tall, muscular, fierce-looking man with a spear in his hand, a sword in his belt, and a plumed, shining helmet tucked under his arm. Yet despite his straight back and broad shoulders, something in his eyes seemed defeated.

He looked slowly around the room until his troubled gaze lighted on Arthur and Finn.

"I was a gladiator," he began. "I fought mostly at the Flavian Amphitheater in Rome. My name was Marcus, and I was an equite."

"Gladiator on a horse," Finn whispered to Arthur.

"My brother..." Marcus began. Finn guessed silently that this would be another mission to avenge someone's death. "My brother died with

Spartacus, you know."

"Your brother and thousands more besides!" said the Professor. "You have our most sincere sympathies, although I doubt we will be able to reverse the outcome of that particular war."

"No, it is true," said the gladiator. "They were destined to lose, but I would not change any of that. My brother died fighting for a principle—for freedom. I had the chance to fight for the same thing, and I ignored it. I chose to stay when he escaped, and I fought on in the arena. I earned my freedom eventually, but along the way I killed many people as a gladiator. I was not fighting for a principle. I was fighting to save my own skin and to entertain the crowds." Marcus paused, his head bent low and his hands gripping the side of the doorway.

"As soon as I heard of my brother's death, I wished that I had escaped with him and fought alongside Spartacus. If there had been more of us, things might have been different..."

"And what would you change about your life if you could?" asked Finn.

"I would take the chance to fight for something real," replied Marcus. "The chance to show nobility, that is all..."

Finn and Arthur exchanged another nervous glance. This was a less specific request than usual, and might be hard to get right. However, Marcus had no more to say. In two long strides, he had crossed the room and placed a hand on each boy's shoulder.

The air in the room shifted and seemed to fill with mist, drifting at first, then whirling faster and faster around them. In moments, the study could no longer be seen, and it felt to the boys as though they were spinning through the sky...

CHAPTER 2

"You're going to get a beating, boy! I said stand up!" Arthur heard the words as though he were listening through a thick wall. As he slowly opened his eyes and began to take in his surroundings, he became sharply aware of a terrible stench filling his nostrils. Looking up, he saw that he was lying in a narrow alleyway, hemmed in by tall buildings.

The stench, he soon realized, came from the mounds of rotting food and sewage that muddied the ground around him.

"Where am I?" Arthur groaned, leaning on one elbow and blinking up at a dusty, orange sky.

"You're on my patch, boy," a harsh voice replied. Arthur twisted around slowly to see a rough, scarred, street-wise looking teenager glaring down at him. The boy was slapping the end of what seemed to be a well-used club into the palm of his hand. "I'm Festus," the boy growled. "And that's all you need to know. Now get up and tell me why you're here or, by Jupiter, I'll crush your skull before you say another word."

Suddenly, Arthur didn't feel so bleary-eyed. He dragged himself quickly to his feet and held his hands up, noticing for the first time that a gang of similarly menacing boys stood behind Festus.

"I...I'm new here. I don't know where I am," Arthur spluttered, still slightly confused and trying to buy time. He held out little hope of out-fighting or out-running the gang.

"You're on my patch, boy," Festus repeated, with a sneer. "This is Rome. Welcome to the greatest city in the world," he added, sarcastically.

"Uh...Thanks," said Arthur, stepping forward warily. "Now if you'll just let me past, I'll be on my way and off your patch."

Festus stood motionless. "What do you think, lads?"

"Let's teach him a lesson," one of the gang called back, and the rest began cheering. Arthur's heart sank. He quickly tried to think of a way out of the situation. Only one idea came to mind, and it was risky. But he couldn't come up with another way out. Taking a deep breath, he puffed out his chest and glared at the gang.

"Cowards!" he shouted.

The cheering stopped instantly. Festus's face darkened, and he stepped a little closer to Arthur.

"You think we're cowards? We'll see who's begging for mercy in a minute, shall we?"

"Well, if you're not a coward, then let's make this a fair fight," said Arthur, praying his challenge would work. "Me against the best you've got. One on one. No weapons. Unless, of course," he added slyly, "you only fight in packs and only when your opponent is unarmed..."

"You don't know what you're doing, boy," Festus growled. "But you asked for it, and you're going to get it. I'll fight you. And by the time I've finished, you'll wish I'd set the whole gang on you instead."

"We'll see," said Arthur, raising his fists. "But if I win, that's it. You let me go."

"Agreed." Festus nodded. "You won't win, though. We won't fight here in an alley. We need some space." He turned his back on Arthur and pushed his way back through the gang. "Bring him to the arena," he barked.

It was only as Arthur found himself being roughly frogmarched along the alley by Festus's gang that he realized his plan had worked.

* * *

Some distance away, Finn sat up in an empty alley and rubbed his eyes, wincing as a foul smell and a loud, metallic banging assaulted his senses. Like Arthur, it always took Finn a few minutes to remember where he was and why he was there when he first woke up in a new time. Looking around for clues, Finn noted that the stinking alley ran between two dismal-looking apartment blocks, at one end of which there seemed to be a lighter, busier, more open space.

He stretched, pushed himself to his feet, and cautiously made his way along the alley, emerging into a very shabby market square. The sides of the square were lined with tables, benches, and grubby wooden shacks, most of which seemed to serve as shops. Other shacks, judging by the raucous voices of the men at the tables, were bars.

Cautiously, Finn began walking around the perimeter of the square, staying in the shadows and trying not to draw attention to himself. After a few moments, his brain cleared. A closer look at the tunics worn by the men in the square instantly reminded him what he was there for. Rome! The gladiator! Freedom!

The satisfaction of remembering their mission was quickly overtaken by a feeling of surprise. This wasn't how Finn expected Rome to look. It looked too...modern. Behind the shops that lined the square, the apartment blocks rose five or six stories up to tiled rooftops.

A shout interrupted his thoughts. "Prepare the arena for Festus!"

An arena? Finn glanced around in confusion, looking for anything that might resemble a gladiator's arena. Some of the men at the tables began cheering and laughing. From an alley on the opposite side of the square, Finn saw a gang of teenagers spilling out past a bar and into the middle of the square.

Where's the arena? Finn wondered. Then he groaned as he saw a smaller boy being marched along, held tight by two of the gang members.

Arthur.

"How does he do this every time?" Finn hissed to himself, furious that his brother had yet again damaged their chances of success by getting into trouble and making a spectacle of himself within minutes of arriving. He watched, dismayed, as Arthur was pushed along into the middle of the square, the gang calling over to the men to join them as they formed a human circle around him. Several of the men put their cups down and obliged. Finn guessed that the "arena" for this gang just meant any piece of open ground where they could fight.

"And who do we have here?" one of the men shouted.

"This little runt challenged Festus to a fight!" one of the gang replied.

Challenged? Finn's stomach tightened.

"Still fighting lambs, eh, Festus? You'll make a great gladiator one day!" the man jeered, and his friends chuckled. It was obvious that Festus was not held in very high regard by the men.

The tough-looking, scarred teenager stepped forward from the circle and turned to face the men. "Lamb or wolf," he growled, swinging a club menacingly. "No one challenges me on my patch and gets away with it!"

"No weapons," Finn heard Arthur call out. "We agreed. Or do you only fight when you have an unfair advantage?"

Finn began to see what had happened. Maybe Arthur hadn't been so stupid after all. Nevertheless, Finn didn't like his brother's chances against this thug.

Scanning the sides of the market square, Finn began to think up a plan to help Arthur escape. He noticed a grizzled giant of a man standing alone in the shadows, observing the gang. Something about him seemed too dangerous to Finn, and he decided against asking him for help. Maybe the drinkers were a better bet. He sidled up next to the man who had taunted Festus, and hoped he would agree to help him.

* * *

"Come on, Festus," one of the gang cheered. "Teach him a lesson."

Arthur looked over at the men who were watching. He grinned, then bleated like a lamb, sending the men into fits of laughter. The more people he could get on his side, the better.

Without warning, Festus hurled his club to the ground and charged at Arthur. Calmly, as if he had known it would happen, Arthur stepped to one side, leaving a foot trailing so Festus tripped and tumbled to the ground. The men cheered and Festus sprang to his feet, snarling. Arthur could see that his opponent was much stronger than him. His only hope was to keep Festus so enraged that he couldn't think clearly. As the thug advanced more carefully toward him, Arthur began dancing sideways around the circle as though he were in a boxing ring, bleating even more comically. Glaring menacingly, Festus crouched low and circled with him, waiting for his chance.

Arthur could see real hatred in Festus's eyes now. The angry boy made mini-lunges toward him, but never broke eye contact. The cheers and laughter of the spectators faded as Arthur focused all his attention on the fight. When the next attack came, it was far more controlled. Festus stepped forward, moved as if to punch Arthur in the stomach, but instead dropped to one knee. Grabbing hold of Arthur's ankle, he give it a vicious twist. Arthur crashed to the ground. Festus pinned him down with an arm across his chest and punched him on the chin.

Ignoring the pain of his bruised chin, Arthur threw his head one way and the other, trying to dodge the blows. Festus pulled his arm right back to deliver the killer punch.

Sensing a shift in the weight across his chest, Arthur slid a few inches to one side. He snapped his head out of the way just as Festus brought his fist down with all his weight behind it. The blow glanced off the side of Arthur's head and thumped into the mud, drawing a cry of pain from Festus, who had followed his own fist to the ground.

Seizing his opportunity, Arthur rolled out from under his opponent and leaped to his feet, aiming a swift kick at Festus's ribs as the older boy pushed himself up.

Festus howled with anger and crashed forward once more, throwing another vicious punch. Arthur weaved to one side, grabbed Festus's wrist in both hands, and twisted. The punch carried the older boy forward and past Arthur.

Now Arthur was in complete control, as he stood behind Festus and twisted his arm up behind his back. He curled a foot in front of Festus and pushed, sending him sprawling. This time, Arthur went down with him, holding Festus by his twisted arm and landing on his back so that the older boy could not move.

The men clapped and cheered, as Festus's gang looked darkly on.

"It's over, Festus!" said the man standing next to Finn, laughing. "You took on the mighty lamb, and the lamb won!"

Arthur looked down at his opponent. "Are we done?"

Festus grunted, and Arthur rolled away.

* * *

Swallowing his nerves, Finn tapped the man next to him on the arm. "Excuse me sir," he said.

"What is it, boy?" the man barked, glancing at Finn for the first time. "You want to have a go, too?"

"No!" Finn replied hurriedly. "I'm no match. But this lamb-boy put up a good fight, didn't he?"

"Not bad," the man nodded. "Not bad at all."

"Then we'll make sure the gang lets him go, sir?"

Before the man could reply, there was a cheer from the gang. Finn turned to see Festus lunge for the club he had thrown to the ground. Roaring, he charged at Arthur once more, swinging wildly.

"*Hey!*" Finn shouted. "*Leave him alone!*"

A few of the gang members turned on Finn and shoved him backward, knocking him into the older man.

"The boy's right," shouted the man. "The lamb won fair and square. Let him go."

"No chance!" Festus yelled.

"Are you going to let them talk to you like that?" Finn egged the man on.

"No," snarled the man. He pushed his way through the gang toward Festus. He was joined by several of the other men. The gang's circle disintegrated, and a brawl broke out. Fists and boots and knees and heads connected with each other.

So many bodies were filling the square now that Finn had to dodge his way through the blows as best he could. He was desperate to reach Arthur, who was struggling to avoid Festus's club.

"I said leave him alone!" Finn shouted, darting forward and leaping onto Festus's back. Festus staggered backward, then crashed to the ground yet again. Arthur rushed forward and stomped on Festus's arm. He dropped the club and roared in pain.

"To me, boys!" Festus called, jumping to his feet and thrashing his elbows around to shake Finn off. Finn just grinned at him.

"It's over, Mr. Wolf," Finn mocked. "Your friends have had enough." They were surrounded now by a ring of the older men. The last of the gang members had scurried and limped away into the alleys. Festus's shoulders slumped.

"Get out of here!" ordered the man who had spoken to Finn. Festus didn't need to be told twice and darted away toward one of the alleys.

Arthur and Finn looked around at the circle of men.

"Thanks!" they both said at once.

It was only then Finn noticed that the giant who had been watching from the shadows earlier had joined the circle of men. The huge brute stepped forward, and the others, also now aware of him, began to inch away.

"You two!" he boomed. "The games begin next week, and I'm looking for fighters. We need to talk."

EXTRACT FROM *WARRIOR HEROES*
BY FINN BLADE

LIVING IN ROME

HOUSING

The population of ancient Rome
was around 800,000, making it by
far the largest city in the world
at that time. Romans would have
led very different lives from those
living elsewhere.

Most people lived in apartments,
and many of the streets were lined
with apartment blocks that were up
to eight stories high. They were
made of wood and bricks, or an
early form of concrete, and had
tiled roofs. But many of them were
built cheaply by greedy landlords,
and many people died when the
buildings collapsed.

SHOPS

In busy streets and market squares, the rooms at the bottom of each block of apartments contained shops and bars, just like cities today.

WATER

The Romans built raised canals called aqueducts to pipe fresh water down into the city from clean rivers in the hills. The clean water fed the public drinking fountains and the public baths.

BATHS

Unless you were very rich, or very poor, you would have used the public baths in Rome. These had steam rooms, swimming pools, and areas for wrestling and games. They were like recreation centers today, but made of marble. Oh, and everyone walked around naked at the baths!

BATHROOMS

Most people also used public
bathrooms. There were no cubicles
for the toilets, so they really were
public! Sewage sloshed away through
underground sewers and out into the
Tiber River.

CHAPTER 3

Arthur yawned and rubbed his shoulder. Three days had passed since Gaius had told them he wanted a new training partner for one of the young gladiators at the school. Gaius was a lanista, or manager, of gladiators. He ruled over them and was responsible for their training. He had been impressed by what he saw when Arthur fought Festus. He had also spotted Finn talking to the men to make sure that Arthur got out alive after winning his fight, and he had asked both boys to come with him to the gladiator school.

Finn had stared around in awe as Gaius led them from Festus's arena, and through the streets of Rome to the gladiator school. No number of history lessons on Rome could have prepared him for the sheer scale of the city. They passed huge victory arches, domed, marble temples, and soaring stone columns with statues perched on top. Clean, oiled men in togas emerged from public baths, and shopkeepers shouted at slaves. In the heat, small groups congregated beside beautiful public drinking fountains. Finn had again found himself marveling at how modern it all felt.

Exactly what Gaius had in mind for Finn remained a mystery. But when they arrived at the compound of the gladiator school, Arthur was set to work immediately, sparring with Gaius and the other trainers.

After his first day of training, Arthur slumped down onto his mattress as soon as he entered his cell. Gaius had put his new recruit through his paces, and Arthur felt more bruised and broken than at any other time in his life. Finn smiled across at him.

"Hard day?"

"It's all right for you!" said Arthur, bitterly. "You haven't had to do anything!"

"Yeah," Finn snorted. "Look at all this luxury! I can do whatever I want." Their tiny room was more like a prison cell than anything else. The two thin mattresses on the floor were the only things in the room.

"At least the stone walls keep us cool, I suppose," Finn went on, trying to find something positive to say about their situation. "Anyway, I can't help it if I'm the brains and you're the brawn. It's going well. We're inside the gladiator school, and it's only a matter of time before we meet Marcus. Then all we have to do is persuade him to fight for his freedom so he dies happy!"

Arthur yawned and stretched out on the mattress. "And when we do finally meet Marcus," he said, "what are we going to say to him?"

Finn paused and furrowed his brow. "I've been thinking about that. It looks like it will probably be you who meets Marcus. And when you do, you may not have much time to talk to him."

"That's if he'll even talk to me at all." There was silence as the boys pondered the challenge they would face. How would they persuade a gladiator who saw them as strangers to plan an escape and fight for his principles? "How will I even make him listen to anything I've got to say?"

"You need to try to establish a connection right away," said Finn. "Persuade him you're not really a total stranger after all. Either that or just get him thinking about his brother–that's what this is all about. Marcus died regretting that he didn't fight for his freedom the way his brother did. It must have played on his mind his whole life. Try to leave Marcus with thoughts of his brother and Spartacus."

"Then what?" said Arthur, looking unconvinced.

"Then we'll have to give him something to

fight for, obviously!"

A loud thump on the door of the boys' cell prevented them talking further. Gaius ducked through the doorway.

"How are the muscles?" he said, flashing Arthur a quick smile. Arthur puffed out his cheeks in exhaustion. Gaius laughed. "You'd better get used to it. Tomorrow you begin sparring with Ajax."

Gaius had already told Arthur about his top young gladiator, Ajax. At fifteen, Ajax was little more than a boy himself. He was scheduled to fight another teenager from the same gladiator school in the public arena the following week.

"I never asked," Arthur interjected. "Who was he sparring with before you found me?"

"There was an accident," said Gaius, matter-of-factly. "We needed someone new, and Ajax needs to learn some control." Arthur's eyes widened and his mouth dropped open. "Finn, come with me. Your work starts tonight."

Casting a nervous glance back at Arthur, Finn got to his feet and followed the huge lanista out of the cell. They crossed the open space of the training arena to a gate in the walls of the compound. Gaius paused at the gate.

"Put this on," he commanded, throwing a cloak at Finn. "And keep the hood up."

"But I'm not cold," Finn protested.

"It's not to keep you warm, boy. It's to keep you hidden. Come, I'll tell you as much as I know on the way."

"On the way where?" Finn asked nervously, wrapping the cloak around his shoulders and pulling up the hood.

"Stop asking questions!" Gaius snapped. "I said I'll explain on the way. Now follow me."

Gaius looked at Finn's hood, grunted with approval and unlocked the gate of the gladiator school. He stepped through the gate and out onto the dark street. They set off briskly and Finn had to run to keep up. All the while, he did his best to memorize their route, as they cut through stinking, muddy alleyways, across squares, and eventually out onto a busier, paved road that seethed with activity. Carts and chariots rumbled along the road. Whips cracked. Crowds jostled. Beggars cried out. But Finn could think of nothing beyond staying close to Gaius.

After what seemed like an eternity, they left the main road. The crowds thinned. Gaius suddenly said, "We're going to see Lucius. Listen and remember. Lucius is a senator. He owns the gladiator school, which means he owns you. Lucius has many rivals in the senate, but there is one man who is a particular threat to him. His name is Titus, and he owns another gladiator school. Lucius believes that Titus plans to have him assassinated. He needs someone loyal to infiltrate Titus's household."

"To do what?" Finn enquired.

"I don't know, boy, that's what we're going to find out. It was not just a sparring partner for Ajax that I was looking for when I found you and your brother. I was looking for someone smart. Someone whose face would not be recognized. Someone who could be a spy."

Finn swallowed dryly. All this was taking him farther and farther away from Arthur and

Marcus, and into seriously dangerous territory. In any case, with no knowledge of Rome, Finn couldn't see how he would be any use as a spy.

Finn's nervousness increased until it finally got the better of him. Before he knew what he was doing, he blurted out, "Wait! There's something you need to know."

Gaius stopped and stared at him steadily.

"I...I'm not from Rome. Arthur and I only just got here. I don't know the streets or the people, or even the customs."

"You think I hadn't noticed that, boy?" Gaius snorted. "But you're smart. Can you remember the way back to the gladiator school?"

Finn thought for a moment, then began to describe the way back.

Gaius nodded. "And you were smart enough

to get a bunch of drunk soldiers on your side to look out for your brother the other day."

"Yes, but..."

"But nothing!" Gaius snapped. "Lucius needs someone with no connections. Someone whose face has never been seen before. He needs someone who will arouse no suspicions. You say you don't know Rome? Well, know this: Rome is a city of thieves and liars, and the greater the rank, the greater the lies. Deep down, every senator fears he will one day be assassinated by a rival, and probably by one who claimed to be a friend. If you were from Rome, Lucius would never be able to trust you."

"But he's never even met me. Why would he ever trust me?"

"I suppose that's why he wants to meet you

tonight," said Gaius. "And, of course, he knows that you care about your brother."

There was no threat in Gaius's tone, but Finn couldn't miss the warning the statement carried. As Gaius set off along the road once more, Finn shivered and followed silently.

As they walked, an intriguing question began to form in Finn's mind. *What happens to Lucius's gladiators if he is assassinated?* Finn had no idea, and he wasn't about to ask. But it seemed to him that the sudden death of Lucius might be the perfect catalyst for an escape attempt by some of his gladiators—or even just one.

"This is the back of the house." Gaius's voice cut into his thoughts. They were standing by a simple door in a high wall, flanked by a pair of sullen-looking guards. "Don't ask questions.

Don't look at Lucius, unless he's talking to you. And don't even think about suggesting you're not up to the job. Is that understood?"

Finn nodded. Gaius muttered something to the guards, who rapped on the door and waved them through when it swung inward.

The contrast between the grubby street and the oasis they entered took Finn's breath away. They were standing in a covered stone walkway that ran around the perimeter of a beautiful, sweet-smelling garden. At one end, stood the most stunning house Finn had ever seen. Through the arches of the walkway, he could make out elegant statues, lush plants, and a magnificent fountain. The sight almost made Finn forget why he was there, and it was a few moments before he noticed that a male slave in a simple tunic stood waiting for them.

"Is your master ready for us?" asked Gaius.

The slave nodded and led the way. They entered the house, and stopped outside an intricately carved door. Finn gazed around at the cool, clean marble as the slave made a coughing sound.

"Enter!" came a thin, high reply.

Finn felt suddenly very aware of all the dangers he and Arthur faced in their quest to help Marcus. Somehow they had to find Marcus and persuade him to escape with two boys he had never even met before. Even worse, Arthur had to survive brutal combat as a gladiator's sparring partner. As for Finn, he was about to meet one of the most powerful men in Rome—the man who owned them all. Finn swallowed hard as Gaius pushed him toward the door.

EXTRACT FROM *WARRIOR HEROES*
BY FINN BLADE

LIFE AS A GLADIATOR

Gladiators were trained and housed in schools by a lanista, who was a bit like a brutal drill sergeant. The lanista had to make sure the gladiators would put on a good show and fight bravely. Gladiators needed expert fighting skills, but they also needed to be tough enough to keep on fighting, even if they were losing or injured. The lanista also had to be sure that if the gladiators were instructed to do so, they would kill their enemy after defeating him. Training was extremely tough!

CELEBRITY

Sometimes the gladiators from a

particular owner would be hired
out for shows in other cities, so the
best gladiators became famous all
over the empire. They were portrayed
in art and literature, and you
can still see some of their names
carved into walls around Rome. Add
the fact that gladiators performed
in huge stadiums in front of fans
cheering out their names, and you
can see why they were the sports
celebrities of their day.

SLAVES

Despite their fame, gladiators
had very low social status because
most were slaves. Some were able to
earn their freedom after years of
surviving battle. These fortunate
few could actually retire wealthy,
since they were often allowed to
keep much of their prize money.

CHAPTER 4

The meeting was brief but highly unsettling. Lucius, a bony, middle-aged man with a cruel mouth, stood in the center of the room, the white cloth of his toga brushing the floor. He studied Finn in silence as Finn stared at the man's sandals.

"Let me see your face," Lucius instructed. Something in the man's tone made Finn's stomach turn as he pulled back his hood.

"He's very young," the senator commented, taking a step forward and grabbing Finn's chin firmly. "Look at me, boy." Finn did as he was told, trying hard to resist the urge to wrench the man's hand aside.

"Do you wish any harm to come to your brother?" Lucius asked quietly, never taking his eyes off Finn's.

Finn swallowed and shook his head.

"Of course not," Lucius went on. "Then do not fail me."

Finn nodded, the power of speech failing him.

"Those who fail me are punished, do you understand, boy?" As he said this, Lucius gestured toward the slave who had shown Finn in. The slave grimaced and opened his mouth. Finn's eyes widened. He couldn't be certain, but it seemed that the boy was missing his tongue. Finn blinked in shock and looked back at Lucius, nodding quickly.

"Good. You may go. Gaius will instruct you soon. Wait for him in the garden."

Finn stumbled back out of the house, his hands over his mouth, and sat down heavily on a stone bench. Grave thoughts and fears whirled in his head. He and Arthur had no plan for an escape attempt with Marcus–they had not even met him yet–and now Marcus's owner was effectively holding Arthur hostage. And what a sinister man. Finn shivered with loathing at the all-too-fresh memory of Lucius's terrible, soft voice in his ear and the image of what failure had cost that slave.

A hand touched his shoulder. Finn jumped off the bench with a hoarse cry, flinging an elbow back as he did so.

He spun around, fists clenched, only to find himself eye to eye with a startled-looking girl.

"I'm sorry," they both said at once, then laughed as a little of the tension evaporated.

"I am Lucilla," said the girl. "My apologies, I shouldn't have surprised you."

"Not your fault," Finn replied. "I'm just a bit distracted at the moment. I'm Finn."

The girl walked around to the front of the bench and sat down, motioning for Finn to do the same.

"Most people are nervous after meeting my uncle. He has that effect on people."

"Your uncle?" Finn gulped, instantly back on guard. Lucilla nodded, forlornly.

"I wish he were not. He is not a good man—but I think you might know that already. You are the boy who will spy on Titus, are you not?"

Finn froze, not sure how to respond.

"I'm not supposed to know, but I make it my business to find out what my uncle is planning when it comes to Titus. I hear that you are not from Rome, so perhaps I can trust you." Lucilla paused. Her face clouded over as she spoke in a low voice, "I am to marry Titus."

"What? How old are you?" Finn blurted, confused. "And isn't Titus your uncle's enemy?"

"I am twelve years old, and yes, Titus and my uncle are rivals. I am a peace offering, I think." Even in the middle of all his own troubles, Finn found himself feeling sorry for Lucilla.

Casting a furtive glance over her shoulder, Lucilla continued briskly, "Listen, we don't have long. I am just asking that if you discover anything that puts my marriage to Titus in doubt, you will get word to me. Marrying Titus will get me away from my uncle, and I have to escape this house one way or another."

"Why?" Finn asked.

Lucilla's face darkened further. "I just have to.

I hate him. If I could kill him without getting caught, I would. But he is very, very careful. He kills anyone who gets in his way. Yet no one seems to be able to kill him. He poisons people. Did you know that? He poisoned my parents."

She was interrupted by the sound of footsteps. Lucilla jumped up quickly from the bench.

"Goodbye for now, Finn," she whispered, and slipped away just before Gaius and the slave emerged from the house.

* * *

An hour later, Finn was standing face to face with Titus, a knot in his stomach. Lucius's instructions could not have been clearer or more sinister: *Kill Titus and Arthur lives.* Gaius had met Finn in the garden after Lucilla had disappeared. He delivered the instruction in a strained voice. He clearly was not happy about something. But whether it was the plan to assassinate Titus or the fact that Lucius was using a boy to do the work, Finn could not tell. Gaius had placed around Finn's neck a cord that had a small bottle hanging from it. Poison—Lucius's weapon of choice, just as Lucilla had said.

As Finn followed Gaius's directions to the villa where Titus lived, he had become more and more certain that the fix for everyone's problems was for Lucius to be killed. Finn didn't like the idea of doing this himself, but he wasn't sure he had much choice.

Lucilla would be free of the terrible uncle who had murdered her parents. Arthur and Finn would be free of the man who was effectively holding them hostage. And Marcus might well be prompted to fight for his freedom, too. It was a risky strategy, but it was the only one that seemed to lead in the right direction. Following this logic, Finn had decided that the only thing he could do was approach Titus with complete honesty. When he arrived at the villa, he announced that he was there to warn Titus about an attempt on his life. He was escorted under guard to a room not unlike the one in which he had met Lucius.

However, the man who stared back at him could not have been more different from Lucius. Tall, strong, and with something noble in his bearing, Titus displayed none of Lucius's menacing appearance. He listened to Finn's explanation of events without interruption. When Finn had finished speaking, Titus continued to look at him thoughtfully.

"Show me the poison," he said at length.

Swallowing nervously, Finn removed the bottle from around his neck and handed it over. Titus removed the stopper and waved the liquid under his nose. He nodded slowly before closing the bottle and placing it on a table. "Let me be sure that I fully understand the facts," he said. "Your brother is in training to be a gladiator. You were recruited to poison me, and told that your brother would pay dearly if you failed. And Lucilla wants to escape Lucius because she knows that he killed her parents."

Finn nodded, praying that he had not

misjudged the situation.

"And you are telling me this because you hope I might help you in return for your honesty."

Finn nodded again.

"Then you are either very brave or very stupid. Or both," said Titus, quietly. He paused.

Finn's heart pounded. Titus studied Finn carefully and continued, "I can see no reason for you to invent any of this, so this is what we will do..."

CHAPTER 5

"Arthur," Gaius called, "It's time."

Stomach lurching, Arthur followed Gaius across the sand to the middle of the training arena. Arthur's fighting skills were impressive. He had fought with Vikings, samurai, knights, and many other kinds of warriors, learning from each of them. But despite training with Gaius, Arthur still did not feel ready to fight a properly trained gladiator—even if they were just supposed to be sparring. He wondered how Finn was doing. Early that morning before he set off, Finn had told him all about the meeting with Lucius and the assassination plot.

"Remember," Gaius called gruffly, interrupting Arthur's worries. "Ajax is a secutor. His weapons and armor are stronger than yours, but they are also heavier. If you show the same speed that you used against Festus the other day, then you can give Ajax a good run. Now, let's check your gear." Gaius nodded as he ran his hands over each of Arthur's light defenses: a shoulder guard, a leg guard, and an arm guard.

"One more thing, Arthur. Ajax is a good fighter, but he has a nasty temper. Just remember this is a sparring bout. Don't end up starting a war. Ajax is fighting for real in the arena tomorrow for the first time. He needs practice today, but I don't want him getting injured. Do you understand?"

Arthur nodded, curling his fingers more tightly around his net and trident. As a retiarius, these were his only weapons, except for the dagger in his belt. As the lanista led him out into the arena, he couldn't help feeling that he was the only one who was going to come out of this bout injured. If what Gaius had implied about Ajax's last sparring partner was correct, then he'd be lucky to get out alive, let alone unscathed.

"Wait here," said Gaius. Arthur looked around the now familiar training arena. Three of the four sides of the compound were lined with long rows of cells, so that the arena was the first thing every gladiator saw when he woke up in the morning. The smooth, dusty compound walls were about twice the height of a man—high enough that you couldn't climb over them, in any case.

Several older gladiators stood watching in the early morning sun. One of them nodded at Arthur and smiled. *Marcus!* Arthur realized with a start. Maybe this was his chance to make contact. But before he could act on his thought, a door opened across the compound. Through it, Arthur caught sight of the gladiator he was about to fight.

He gulped. If Ajax was fifteen, then he was a monster. He was massive, even next to the huge, curved, rectangular shield he carried. A smooth, bronze helmet covered his whole head and face, the gleaming metal broken by two small eye holes in which Arthur could see only darkness. Ajax looked like some sort of demonic warrior from a nightmare. Arthur shuddered, suddenly very aware of the air on his unprotected face as Ajax swung his heavy sword through the air in huge circles.

"Now, boys," Gaius instructed. "You're only sparring, but I want a proper fight just the same. Until I say stop, you keep fighting, and you fight to win. The instant I say stop, you stop. Any repeat of last time, Ajax, and I'll have you whipped. Do I make myself clear?"

The lanista broke off and turned as he heard footsteps behind him. "Lucius, sir. This is an unexpected honor."

Arthur tried hard not to stare at the man

Finn had spoken of with so much loathing the previous night.

"Carry on!" said Lucius, and he flicked his hands at the boys. "Final preparations for the bouts taking place today and tomorrow, eh, Gaius? I thought I would come and inspect my gladiators before our moment of glory arrives. I see Marcus is looking well. Come here, man."

Marcus walked obediently forward. Lucius placed a hand on the gladiator's arm. Arthur got the impression that Marcus was gritting his teeth.

"You will do me proud this afternoon, eh, Marcus? A fine specimen like you. It is on days such as these that a gladiator repays his master in glory." Lucius said with a simpering smile.

"I am here to serve, master," Marcus replied

stiffly, staring straight ahead.

"Quite so," said Lucius. "You are all here to serve me and the citizens of Rome. And where is our latest recruit, Gaius? The boy?"

Arthur groaned inside as Gaius guided Lucius in his direction.

"My dear Gaius," Lucius snorted, squeezing Arthur's arm. "He really is just a boy isn't he?"

"He can fight, sir."

"Well," said Lucius, looking long and hard at Arthur. "I'll have to take your word. Let us hope that no significant harm befalls him, eh? I see that Ajax is looking primed and ready as ever. What a find he was. Mark my words, Gaius. Ajax has a glorious future ahead of him, and it begins in the arena tomorrow. He will become one of the greats, I am sure of it. Well, let us see the action, then. On with the fight!" Lucius clapped his hands together, and with a whirl of his toga, positioned himself a safe distance away from the boys.

"Very well, sir. Ajax, Arthur, the fight begins and ends at my command. Is that understood?" Arthur nodded. Ajax, still staring at Arthur through his helmet, crouched slightly and raised his sword arm, ready to strike.

Arthur tested the weight of the net in his hand. He had spent hours with Gaius learning how to cast the net at an opponent to ensnare them, but now that he was facing a fully armed gladiator for the first time, it felt like a feeble weapon. The trident in his other hand was more reassuring. Its length meant that he should be able to keep Ajax at a safe distance.

Slowly, Ajax began to advance. Arthur felt the familiar rush of blood and adrenaline that always came over him when he was fighting–which was far too often these days for his liking. His opponent was far better protected than he was, thanks to the shield and helmet, but they looked heavy. Arthur, on the other hand, could move about freely and lightly. Gaius had said in an actual fight a retiarius might try to win by making the secutor

chase after him for a long time, draining the heavily weighed-down secutor of energy. But the training arena was not big enough for that.

Ajax was a short distance away now, just out of reach of Arthur's trident. Arthur sprang into action, taking a step forward and jabbing with the trident. It clattered into Ajax's shield and glanced off. Arthur's momentum took him a step closer to the gladiator. He had to twist awkwardly away as Ajax thrust at him with his sword.

Heart pounding, Arthur retreated a few steps. Once more, Ajax began to advance. Arthur threw the net at Ajax's head, then watched in horror as it slid off the smooth helmet and landed on the ground behind his enemy. One weapon lost, Arthur switched the trident to his left hand just as Ajax lunged forward, holding his shield out before him like a battering ram. Ajax crashed into Arthur, who fell heavily to the ground, trapping the trident beneath his own weight.

Ajax towered over him, shield discarded and sword raised in a two-handed grip, ready to plunge it into Arthur. Horrified, Arthur snatched the only weapon remaining in his belt—a dagger.

"Enough!" Gaius called, but Ajax paid no heed.

He's going to do it! thought Arthur, panic coursing through his body. Sure enough, the sword began to fall. Arthur slashed out with the dagger in the direction of Ajax's feet, and he felt the blade jar against something hard. His opponent howled in pain, dropping his sword and falling to the ground.

"*I said enough!*" Gaius roared.

Arthur sprang to his feet and retreated away from Ajax, as the lanista rushed over to inspect the fallen gladiator.

"Is he injured?" Lucius whined, worried more for the prize money he might lose than the fighter himself. "Can he still fight tomorrow?"

"I fear not, sir." Gaius shook his head grimly, as Ajax writhed on the ground.

"But we have promised a fight between two young gladiators!" Lucius shouted, his temper flaring. "Am I to look a fool before all of Rome? You–boy!" he spat, turning to Arthur. "You are responsible for this outrage, so you will fight in Ajax's place."

"He is not ready, sir," Gaius cautioned.

"Do not question me, Gaius! I have made my decision. The boy stabs my finest young gladiator in the foot. He thinks he can fight, so tomorrow he fights before all of Rome. The idiot has cost me dearly, and he must clear the debt with a great fight tomorrow or else pay the debt with his life."

Arthur felt the blood draining from his head, as the words sank in and the adrenaline cleared. This was getting wildly out of control. The training arena had been terrifying enough, but fighting at the center of the amphitheater in the real arena—and in front of the Roman public? Arthur shivered.

"Steady, boy." Marcus had come over to stand beside Arthur, and now he called over to Gaius. "Shall I take the boy away while you tend to Ajax, master?"

Gaius grunted his consent, as a furious Lucius

turned and swept across the arena toward the main gates.

"Come with me," said Marcus, quietly. He steered Arthur away from his injured foe and back to his cell.

"You're a smart fighter," said Marcus, as Arthur collapsed, shaking, onto his mattress. "For a boy, that is. But they are not right to put you into the arena. You were right to strike at Ajax's feet. He would have killed you, anyone could see that. Lucius is a viper. He has no sense of honor."

"I know how to fight," said Arthur, looking up from his bed. He tried to pull himself together enough to seize this opportunity with Marcus. "Not just fighting for sport like this, either. Fighting for something real. Fighting for freedom."

"Careful, boy. You can say that to me, but if anyone else hears, you could pay with your life. Ever since the slave Spartacus began his uprising, those in charge have been very nervous about gladiators and the idea of freedom."

But Arthur continued, knowing this might be his only chance to speak with Marcus. "I've met a lot of warriors, you know. That's how I know how to fight. But the best I ever met was a man who fought alongside Spartacus. He died in the end, but what a hero. What a way to die. Fighting to be free instead of doing your master's bidding, like a dog. Haven't you ever wanted to do that?"

Marcus gave Arthur a long stare. He nodded. "You remind me of my brother," he said sadly. "There is truth in what you say. But for now, your only worry should be this—surviving the arena."

EXTRACT FROM *WARRIOR HEROES* BY FINN BLADE

GLADIATOR TYPES

To make the fights more interesting, gladiators were trained up to be a certain type of fighter who would wear specific types of armor and use specific weapons. This meant that the organizers could pair types of gladiators together, knowing they were evenly matched. There were many gladiator types. Here are three different kinds.

EQUITE

An equite was a gladiator who rode a horse in the arena, just like the mounted cavalryman in the Roman army. He wore a round helmet with a metal grille across his face, a spear that could be used as a lance or to throw, a short sword, and a small round shield. Equites only ever fought other equites in the arena.

RETIARIUS

The easiest gladiator to recognize was the retiarius because he wore very little armor and no helmet or shield. On the plus side for him, it meant he could run faster. He carried a long trident in one hand and a net in the other, with a dagger in his belt. The trident was used for jabbing, and occasionally throwing, while the net was used either to tangle his opponent or snatch his weapon away.

SECUTOR

A secutor only ever fought in the arena with a retiarius. He had a helmet that covered his entire head, with two eye holes that offered him a very limited view of his opponent. The helmet was smooth on top and unlikely to get snagged in a net, but it was also quite heavy and quickly sapped the wearer's energy. The secutor also carried a large, curved shield and a sword.

CHAPTER 6

Finn stopped, his mouth gaping in awe as a noisy crowd pushed past him in the hot afternoon sun. The massive amphitheater towered above him, a huge monument to Rome's power, and to fighting. The Professor had told Finn that the Flavian Amphitheater, or Colosseum, was built for gladiatorial combat. But standing before it now, Finn could hardly believe his eyes. It looked more like a huge, round palace than a building dedicated to sport. The idea that this vast, beautiful building at the center of the city was built specifically so the citizens of Rome could watch people kill one another was sickening. Yet, he found himself getting caught up in the crowd's excitement.

Tearing his eyes away from the great building, Finn could see Titus and his associates making their way through one of the entrances. Finn quickly darted after them. They had agreed he would enter the amphitheater alone, so that as few people as possible saw them together. He dashed over to the entrance, waving the ticket that Titus had given him at a harassed-looking attendant. Then he jostled through a narrow passage, hopping up and down to keep Titus in view over the heads of the crowd in front of him.

Remembering Titus's directions, he climbed the steps of the amphitheater to the third tier. Since Titus had no gladiators fighting in the games that day, his seats would be higher up, farther away from the action than Lucius.

He climbed the steps until he found the row that his ticket indicated. He walked along it, eyes down, hood up, until he reached his numbered seat. He resolved not to look at Titus, nor look for Lucius, nor even look at the people sitting on either side of him for the first few minutes. He hoped that any curiosity people felt about him would disappear as soon as the spectacle began.

Finn had been expecting a bloodthirsty atmosphere, but everyone seemed very cheerful.

Musicians at the edge of the arena were playing a catchy, upbeat tune that carried loudly around the amphitheater, making the mood of the place festive. People around Finn chatted and joked, shared snacks, and talked about the scheduled fights for that afternoon, as well as the executions they had witnessed earlier in the day. He heard Marcus mentioned more than once, though still had no idea when he would be fighting.

As he waited, Finn went over the plan that he and Titus had agreed on the previous night. Finn had to find a way of appearing to pour the poison into something Titus would then consume. Titus would then give Finn five minutes to exit the amphitheater before collapsing and being carried off by his companions, shouting that he had been poisoned. Finn would head back to Lucius's villa and wait for him there to make sure that the show had been noticed.

Though the scheme was dangerous, Finn was reasonably confident that this part of it would go smoothly. It was the next phase that really worried him. The poison Lucius had provided was supposed to kill very quickly, and Titus would need to appear dead by the time he got home. But Titus was not willing to continue the pretense for long, and had told Finn that he had twenty-four hours to dispose of Lucius one way or another.

It was this part of the plan where Finn's nerves hit a wall. Was he really willing to kill Lucius? Could he poison someone, even if it was a man who deserved it? Finn pushed the problem into the back of his mind, as he had been doing ever since the plan had been hatched. He would just have to see what opportunities arose once he was back at Lucius's villa.

A roar from the crowd interrupted his anxious thoughts, and he looked down at the arena to see the last thing he had expected. A man dressed in a chicken costume was parading around the arena, waving at the crowd!

Wrapped up in an assassination plot at the center of ancient Rome, waiting for the gladiator games to begin, Finn was caught completely off guard by this oddly familiar sight. *I could be at a soccer game*, he thought to himself, chuckling. Someone else in a wolf costume bounded into the arena and started chasing the chicken, accompanied by music and roars of laughter from the crowd. The chase continued for a few minutes, before the wolf caught the chicken and dragged it back down one of the tunnels that led away from the arena.

The music stopped, and after a drum roll, an official began to call out an announcement. But as Finn's eyes sought the announcer out, they came to rest on something that brought the reality of his situation back into focus.

Staring straight back at him from several rows down was the man he knew he would have to kill. Lucius held his gaze for a few moments, then turned and sat down. Had there been something knowing in Lucius's stare? Finn bit his lip anxiously. Lucius couldn't know that Finn and Titus were planning to turn the tables on him, could he?

All of a sudden, Finn jumped as a loud bang

was followed by the clattering of hooves, and two gladiators on horseback cantered into the arena. Both were armed with long spears and small shields, with swords in their belts.

"Our entertainment today begins with a duel between two equites, and for your entertainment, their owner Lucius has stated that they may fight to the death," the caller announced to gasps from the crowd. "On the white horse, making his first appearance in the Flavian Amphitheater, Achilles!" The crowd cheered and clapped as Achilles, dressed in a white tunic to match his white horse, cantered around the edge of the arena with his spear held aloft.

"And on the black horse, needing no introduction to the people of this city, victorious in every bout he has fought, famed across the empire, and here today to fight gloriously once again for the citizens of Rome..." the caller drew breath and threw back his head, "*Marcus!*"

The crowd screamed their approval as Finn got his first look at the man he was here to help, or at least as much of him as could be seen beyond his helmet. Marcus trotted slowly around the arena, his calm bearing as menacing as his black horse and tunic.

Finn had expected to find the games disturbing, but as the thousands of people in the amphitheater rose to their feet and began chanting Marcus's name, Finn found himself on his feet, too. He was caught up with everyone else in anticipation of the fight to come.

Arthur would love this, he thought, wondering what it must be like to have a stadium full of people chanting your name before you begin mortal combat with another warrior. If a gladiator was a champion like this, Finn could see why he might not want to escape. Yet Marcus did not appear to revel in the attention. He seemed calm, still, and centered, in stark contrast to Achilles, who was twisting around in his saddle, tensing and re-tensing his muscles as though fighting something already.

"Gladiators, to the tunnels!" came the call. The two men rode off in opposite directions, and disappeared out of the arena into two different tunnels, heavy doors closing behind them. A slow, heavy drumbeat began, and the crowd fell quiet. The drums grew louder and louder, the sound booming fiercely around the arena, until Finn could feel it pounding in his chest.

His pulse quickened. The crowd stared down expectantly. The doors snapped open again, the crowd bellowed, and the riders galloped out of the tunnels toward one another, covering the distance to the middle of the arena in a flash with arms bent and spears held at shoulder height. Both thrust forward as they came together and both parried with their shields, clattering off one another and slowing as they reached the opposite sides of the arena again. They circled clockwise and the noise from the crowd dipped a little, then rose again as Achilles made the first move and began his charge. Marcus responded immediately, and again the riders tore across the arena to crash spears against shields, and again, neither rider fell.

Again and again they charged, each time to

a roaring crescendo from the crowd, until at last, Marcus caught Achilles with a glancing blow to the shield arm, drawing blood from his opponent and frenzied shouts of encouragement from the crowd. Achilles was knocked back in his saddle, but stayed on his horse and wheeled around immediately to face Marcus again.

This time, Marcus charged and Achilles waited for him. Sensing a climax, the crowd cheered Marcus forward, but Achilles had a surprise in store. When Marcus was still some distance away, Achilles threw his spear. The black horse reared up as the spear sailed past its nose. Twisting out of the spear's path, Marcus fell heavily onto the sand of the arena. Achilles leaped off his horse as Marcus staggered to his feet, casting his spear to one side. Both men drew their swords and rushed to clash again, this time on foot.

The blades flashed in the fierce sunlight. As they met, each blow rang out around the arena, drawing gasps, cheers, and groans from the audience. Achilles, who was apparently unknown to the crowd, was swiftly earning their respect as he matched Marcus blow for blow. It was a frenzied duel, neither man giving or taking any chance to slow the action. Finn felt sure that it would have to end soon.

It suddenly occurred to him that if Marcus were killed, he and Arthur would have failed in their mission to help his ghost—something that had never happened before in all their adventures. *What would happen then? Would they be stuck in Rome forever?*

But he need not have worried. The wound

in Achilles's arm was beginning to take its toll on the gladiator, and Marcus began to beat him back toward the edge of the arena. Moments later, Achilles was down on one knee, fending off overhead blows. One particularly savage strike smashed the sword from his grip. Achilles lifted one arm in the air with a forefinger extended, signifying his surrender. The crowd went wild.

It dawned on Finn that this would be a good moment to make his move, while the crowd was so pumped up. He scurried along the row of seats to his left, in the direction Titus was sitting.

"The victory belongs to Marcus!" cried the announcer, as Finn caught sight of his conspirator.

"And what of Achilles?" the announcer went on. The crowd cheered and called Achilles's

name, clearly impressed by the strength he had shown.

"Will he live or will he die?" Down on the floor of the arena, Finn saw Marcus standing over Achilles, sword still raised.

"Live! Live! Live!" chanted the crowd, as Finn brushed past the last few people separating him from Titus.

"The people have spoken. Achilles lives!"

A great cheer went up, and at that moment, Finn bumped heavily into Titus. He reached a hand out as if to steady himself, grabbing Titus's wrist just above a cup that he was holding.

"Get away!" Titus shouted, pushing him roughly back in the direction he had come from. Finn did as he was told, retreating back toward his seat. He glanced down at Lucius, and met his stare once more. Titus was shouting obscenities after him. Although he could not be sure, Finn thought he saw a smile flicker across Lucius's face.

EXTRACT FROM *WARRIOR HEROES* BY FINN BLADE

A DAY AT THE GAMES

Games at the arena were advertised on billboards around the city. Programs were sold announcing the schedule for the day, which usually went something like this:

- Bestiari - gladiators vs wild animals

- Executions of criminals or duels between prisoners of war

- Bouts between gladiators

The games were a way for the wealthy and powerful to show their generosity toward the public, and keep them on their side, so they were almost always free to attend.

The day would often begin with
some kind of performance and music,
and the crowd would often be given
treats to eat.

THE BIG STAGE

The arenas were sandpits
about the size of a soccer field,
surrounded by rising circular
rows of seats, just like sports
stadiums today. The most famous was
the Flavian Amphitheater, or the
Colosseum, as we know it today. This
huge building in the center of Rome
could hold more than 50,000 people
and was built specifically for the
purpose of holding gladiator games.

CHAPTER 7

The nervous excitement Finn felt at having pulled off the first part of the plan wore off the further he got from the amphitheater. As he approached Lucius's villa, the question he had been avoiding rose again in his mind. Could he really poison someone? It was one thing to defend yourself against an attacker in the heat of battle, but quite another to plan a cold-blooded, secretive assassination. That felt more like...well...murder.

On the other hand, Lucius had more or less threatened to kill both him and Arthur, and it was hard to imagine Marcus suddenly deciding that he wanted to escape, unless something dramatic happened. Also, Finn was worried about Arthur. He knew that deep down his brother was loving pretending to be a gladiator, but the more time he spent in Gaius's school, the more likely it was he would be seriously hurt, whether Lucius was involved or not.

By the time Finn arrived at the villa, he still didn't know what he was going to do beyond telling Lucius that Titus had been poisoned. He went to the small side door he and Gaius had used the previous evening, and one of the guards accompanied him into the courtyard, calling out for the silent slave. The slave appeared and motioned for Finn to follow him. They entered the house and made their way to the room where Finn had first met Lucius. Finn sat down on a bench and waited, staring with loathing at a bust of Lucius that decorated a small alcove.

It wasn't long before another disturbing idea presented itself to him. If Lucius did believe that Titus was poisoned, then what use was Finn to him? In fact, wasn't it in Lucius's interest to get rid of Finn altogether, thereby destroying the evidence?

Just at that moment, the door to the room swung open. Finn held his breath, then sighed with relief when Lucilla walked in.

She made her way quickly over to where he was sitting. "What happened?" she asked, hardly daring to whisper.

Finn, grateful to have one person he could confide in, told her the whole story of his instructions to poison Titus, and of the plot to fool Lucius into believing this had happened. The girl listened carefully, and when he had finished, she thought for a while.

"So Titus was willing to help as long as you dispose of Lucius quickly?"

"That's how he put it, yes, but what am I going to do?" said Finn miserably. "The only plan that makes sense is to kill him, and I don't know if I can do it." As soon as the words were out of his mouth, Finn regretted them. How could he have been so stupid as to say that in this place, and to Lucilla of all people?

"Give me the poison," said Lucilla, her face drawn. "I will do it."

Finn couldn't believe what he was hearing.

"I hate him and I want revenge," she hissed. "And if he lives, then I will have to stay here with him. Now I know that the marriage to Titus was never going to happen, based on what you've told me."

"It's too dangerous," said Finn, his brow creased.

"Finn, you have played your part. Now give me the poison and get back to your brother. What do you think my uncle's plans will be for you, now that he thinks you've done his dirty work? He's ruthless, Finn. He kills anyone he sees as a threat."

Finn knew she was right. Even so, it felt very strange as he pulled the bottle from around his neck and handed it over.

* * *

When Gaius brought Marcus back to the school at the end of the day, Arthur was relieved to learn that the gladiator had won his bout. Arthur had been practicing with his net and trident on and off for most of the day. He hoped with all his heart that somehow Lucius would change his mind about sending Arthur into the arena for the bout that Ajax had been scheduled to fight the following day. But Arthur had seen and heard enough of the cruel senator by then to know that this was unlikely. By his own reckoning, there were only two ways he was going to escape fighting–and probably dying–in the arena. If Titus and Finn's plot had worked, then there was a slim chance that Lucius would be dead by now. Otherwise, the only realistic chance he had was to appeal to Marcus's sense of honor and to his belief that it was unfair to make an untrained boy fight in the arena. And somewhere in there, Arthur would also have to persuade Marcus to escape Rome...tonight.

Gaius had summoned all the trainees and

gladiators in the school to the training arena to hear him announce the day's winners and losers. There were cheers for the victors, but little emotion was spared for those who had died. Arthur got the sense that nobody wanted to think about the reality of gladiators dying in the arena, even though it was something that must have haunted all of them constantly.

After the formality of these announcements, the men were told to wash and prepare themselves for a feast that Lucius would be providing. Thinking quickly, Arthur dashed across to Marcus before he could disappear.

"Congratulations!" he said. "You won!"

"I always do," Marcus replied, simply. "I thought of you today, Arthur, and there is something I want to show you. Go and wait in your cell.

I will be there soon."

Arthur fizzed with energy. This was his first real chance to talk with Marcus of escape. His excitement mounted further when he found Finn back at the cell. In hoarse whispers, the brothers filled each other in on the day's events. Arthur's eyes widened at the news that Lucilla was planning to kill her uncle, and Finn's jaw tightened when he heard that Lucius intended to make Arthur fight in the amphitheater. Finn quickly agreed that they must somehow persuade Marcus to escape with them that night. When the gladiator stooped to enter the cell, they were primed and ready.

Arthur introduced his brother, and Finn explained that he had been in the amphitheater and had seen Marcus fight.

"I heard that you two were brothers," said Marcus. "But I thought it strange that we never saw you training. Why has Gaius brought you here, if not to fight? They are usually happy enough to separate families."

The brothers looked at one another nervously, not sure how much to divulge. Finn shrugged.

"I have chosen to be honest with two people already, and they have helped me," he began. Keeping his voice low, Finn told his story again. Marcus listened intently, his brow furrowing when Finn told him that Lucius had adopted Lucilla after murdering her parents, and further still, at the news that Lucius wanted to use Finn as an assassin.

For a long time after Finn had finished, Marcus said nothing. The boys began to worry that they had misjudged the situation and made a mistake in being so open.

But then Marcus spoke. "Let us hope that the girl succeeds in ridding us of this sick animal. The world will be a better place without him. What sort of man sends boys to kill his rivals? What sort of man kills a child's parents, then tries to become her father? And what sort of man sends an untrained youth into the arena to fight with gladiators? He has no honor. Nor do thousands of others like him in Rome. My brother was right..."

He paused and put a hand to his chest. Something hung from a cord around his neck, and he pulled it over his head. In his open palm, the boys saw a tiny wooden carving of a warrior on horseback.

"I, too, had a brother once," he went on slowly. "He was some years younger than me when we were sold into slavery. I was fully grown when a lanista spotted me and bought me to train as a gladiator. By luck, I was able to persuade him that my brother was also destined to be a fighter. He took a chance and bought my brother, too, although he was not much older than you, Arthur. The first day that I fought in the arena, my brother gave me this carving for luck, and I have never lost. There is something very special between brothers who really believe in each other." He paused, looking at the ceiling.

"I was always the better fighter, but he had the bigger heart. When news reached us of Spartacus, my brother saw something that I did not. He saw a chance to live as a free man.

But I saw only certain death." Marcus shook his head. "We argued and argued. Eventually, I made him swear that he would not join Spartacus. He swore, but I could see in his eyes that it went against everything in his spirit. I woke one morning to find him gone. Years later, I learned that he had become one of Spartacus's most trusted soldiers. I knew then that he must be dead, and ever since that day, I have cursed myself for not knowing him better. I should never have made him swear to stay. It should have been the other way around. I should have been encouraging him to reclaim his freedom. Perhaps I should even have gone with him... And now I learn that the man who *claims* to own me is even more of a monster than I already knew."

"Marcus," said Finn quietly. "Your life isn't over,

you know. You can't bring your brother back, but you can stand up to Lucius. You can help us stop him. And you can follow your brother in spirit by escaping with us and living as a free man somewhere. We have to escape. Arthur is not ready to fight in the arena, and I...I am as good as dead, if Lucius lives."

Marcus stared at Finn, his eyes burning.

"Come with us," insisted Finn. "Honor your brother. Come with us and help two brothers escape and survive together."

There was fire in Marcus's eyes as he opened his mouth to reply. But the words died on his lips, as the door to the boys' room opened. Gaius entered, followed by a thinly smiling Lucius and an ashen-faced Lucilla.

CHAPTER 8

Marcus and the boys jumped to their feet immediately.

"Excellent, excellent," Lucius drawled. "I thought I should congratulate Marcus personally before the feast. I confess, I am surprised to find you here, Marcus. These boys are far beneath the standing of a champion like you, surely! But no matter," he went on, clearly not expecting a reply. "I have something to discuss with the boys, also." His eyes narrowed as he said this. Lucilla stood behind him with a desperate expression on her face meant to warn Finn.

"Finn, you were there to witness Marcus win yet another bout in the arena. Magnificent, was he not? Of course, you will also have the pleasure of watching your brother in combat tomorrow before the citizens of Rome. Although one does sense that his chances of victory are not high."

"But I did as you–"

"Silence!" Lucius hissed. Behind him, Lucilla shook her head frantically. "Your brother has a debt to pay. He injured Ajax, one of my finest. The young brute may never fight again for all we know." He looked at Arthur. "The boy has to pay."

"Sir, the people will not look favorably on an unfair match," Gaius remarked.

"The match will be fair enough," Lucius replied, sneering at Finn. "What could be fairer than a fight between two brothers?"

An eerie silence filled the cell, as everyone stared at Lucius.

"But I did what you told me to do!" Finn blurted.

"You did no such thing!" Lucius screamed, lashing out and slapping Finn hard across the mouth. Finn reeled backward in pain and shock.

"Titus is no closer to death than he was yesterday, whatever your little ruse may have suggested," Lucius snarled. "And do not try to deny it. I have sources close to Titus. Did you—a wretch we picked out of the gutter—did you really think that I would not find out? I have disposed of more enemies and lived through more attempts on my life than you can know!

"You did not poison Titus," Lucius whispered. "He feigned his own death to deceive me, which means that he is plotting something, and you are part of the plot, no doubt. Well, we will see what to do with you," he looked straight at Arthur, "if you survive in the arena tomorrow. But it will be a fight to the death. I promise you that." Lucius paused to appreciate the looks of horror on the boys' faces.

"Now," he went on. "In case you have plans for that poison, where is the bottle?"

"I don't have it," Finn replied.

"It was not used today, so where is it?" Lucius roared, leaping forward and grabbing Finn

by the throat. Marcus stepped toward them, but was ordered back with a barked command from Gaius, who had drawn his sword. Finn shook his head as his ears started to ring.

"Tell me or I will kill you now!"

"Stop!" Lucilla cried. "Stop it. I have the poison, Uncle. And it was I who intended to use it...to give you the death that you have given so many others. Only I had the courage to try to do it myself, and not find someone else to do it for me, like you have done countless times before!"

Lucius dropped Finn like a stone and spun around, his face white with fury.

"I should have killed you when I killed your parents," he spat, as his hand closed around the girl's throat.

"No matter," Lucius snarled, as Lucilla choked under his grip. "There is still time for me to correct my mistake."

"Sir, not the girl–" began Gaius.

"Hold your tongue, fool! It was you who brought the boy to me. For all I know, you are part of the plot."

Lucilla clutched at her uncle's hand, a look of panic spreading across her face. Marcus could hold back no longer. He leaped at Gaius, and with one punch, laid him out cold on the floor.

"Let her go or you die, Lucius," he growled, picking up the lanista's sword.

"Kill *me*?" Lucius howled with laughter. "A gladiator and a slave would dare to kill a senator of Rome? This little scorpion planned to kill me, you heard–"

His words turned to a high-pitched scream as Marcus lunged and thrust forward expertly, burying his sword in Lucius's side. The girl fell gasping to the floor. Marcus braced his foot on the senator and shoved him off the sword. Lucius lay on the floor wheezing and whimpering, clutching at his wound until he became completely still. Lucilla dragged herself to her feet, looked down at her uncle, and spat, before staggering backward and falling against a wall.

Finn and Arthur were too stunned to speak. Marcus acted instantly, instructing them to wait in the cell while he fetched what they would need to flee. He strode away before they could argue. The next to regain his composure, Arthur looked around for something to tie Gaius's hands with.

"We won't have much chance if he wakes up while Marcus is away," he explained, removing the lanista's belt and binding it tightly around the big man's wrists.

"He...What..." Lucilla stammered, staring down at Lucius's motionless body. "He's dead. What will we do?"

"We run," said Arthur. "We get out of Rome with Marcus before the body is discovered.

Gaius heard everything, and he was loyal to Lucius, although I don't think he liked him very much."

"Nobody liked him," Lucilla agreed, bitterly. "But if a senator is killed, someone has to pay. How do we know Marcus has not already accused us?"

But at that moment, Marcus reappeared with a bundle of cloaks and swords for each of them. He stepped briskly into the cell.

"Freedom, you say?"

EXTRACT FROM *WARRIOR HEROES*
BY FINN BLADE

ORIGINS OF THE GLADIATORS

SACRIFICE

The idea of making two people
fight to the death in front of a
crowd wasn't actually Roman in
origin. The Greeks did it, and so
did the Etruscans, who lived near
Rome more than 2,500 years ago. The
Etruscans made people fight to the
death as a sacrifice at funerals.
The Romans picked up the idea and
ran with it.

FUNERALS

It became fashionable for wealthy
Roman families to organize these
funeral duels, and soon, people
started getting carried away. The

spectacle grew and grew. At the biggest funerals for very wealthy people, there could be more than fifty duels.

PUBLIC SPECTACLES

These funeral games were usually played out in public places such as fields and market squares, where you might see a carnival today. The Romans developed a serious appetite for watching people kill each other, so they began to build huge stadiums that allowed thousands of people to watch the games.

BLOODLUST

Eventually, fighting became such big business, and a good gladiator could make so much money for his owner, that it wasn't in anyone's interest to have gladiators kill each other anymore. Of course, the public still wanted to see some blood. To satisfy them, the Romans executed prisoners, or got prisoners of war to fight to the death before the gladiator bouts began later in the day.

CHAPTER 9

As they stood at the gates of the gladiator school looking into the fading evening light, the group of four pulled their hoods up over their heads and checked that their swords were secure under their cloaks. Marcus had told some of the other gladiators that he and the boys had been instructed to take Lucilla back to her father's villa, and that

Gaius and Lucius had some business to discuss before the feast began.

"We have little time," Marcus muttered. "They will be after us soon enough, and we must hurry. We will make for the Tiber, and bribe a boatman to take us along the river and out of the city overnight. With luck, we will be out of Rome before the search is on." But even as Marcus said this, a shout went up inside the school.

"Follow me," Marcus barked. *"Run!"* They dashed after him, heading toward the center of the city.

"They're coming," Finn cried hoarsely, as Gaius and a small group of gladiators spilled out into the street behind them. The fugitives dodged past pedestrians and carts, and sprinted onto a bigger road, drawing stares and curses from the people they passed. This only made the people ahead of them begin to turn and stare, too. Farther along the road, two mounted soldiers turned to see what the commotion was about.

"Urban guards!" Lucilla gasped. "Marcus, I know somewhere we can hide." Marcus nodded and the girl took the lead, darting off the main road and into one of the labyrinth of alleyways. The group shoved past beggars and night-hawkers, twisting and turning through the stinking alleys until Finn and Arthur were completely lost. They could only follow blindly, praying that Lucilla was right. She stopped outside an unmarked door and banged on it with her fist, leaning her head against the wood and gasping for air.

"We don't have long," Marcus warned. They

could not hear any pursuers, but their flight had hardly gone unnoticed.

"I wondered when I'd run into you boys next," someone said from behind them in the dark. Arthur's shoulders sank at the familiar voice.

"Festus," he said, wearily as they all turned around. "Of course, it had to be you."

"We've got a score to settle, boy!" said Festus. The gang behind him muttered their approval.

"Well, you can settle it with me," Marcus growled, stepping in front of Arthur. The change in Festus's expression was almost comical.

"You're...You're a gladiator, aren't you?" Festus couldn't disguise the awe in his voice. "You're Marcus, the equite! I saw you fight today!"

"Then you know better than to pick a fight with my friends."

"These are your friends?" said Festus, astounded, and Marcus seized the initiative.

"I have a proposition for you," he said. "How would you and your gang of kids here like to say one day that you helped a gladiator fight his way out of Rome?"

* * *

An hour had passed by the time they were ready. It came as no surprise that Festus was a huge fan of all gladiators and had watched Marcus fighting in the arena on numerous occasions. Festus and the gang were all too happy to forego their grudge against Arthur if it meant they could help one of their heroes. He had led the fugitives to a small, empty house, where they had hidden in a dark room while he went to arrange for a boat on the Tiber. Festus took a bag of coins with him that Marcus had handed over.

Finn had expressed serious doubts about trusting Festus, but Marcus and Lucilla agreed that there was no choice. The urban guards would be looking for them all over the city by now, and unless they were to split up, which none of them wanted, they would need all the help they could find to get out of Rome alive.

"Giving him money was a mistake," said Finn.

"What choice did we have?" Marcus replied. I had to give him money to buy us a boatman willing to take the risk. In any case, I've won enough bouts in the arena that I am not short of money. I can afford to lose some."

A grinding noise outside the house made

everyone jump, but Arthur peered through a crack in the door, and soon reassured them. It was just Festus, accompanied by one of his gang hauling a cart along the alley.

"We have a plan that should work," Festus announced, proudly. "It's dark now, and there is a boat waiting for you. The guards are searching for four people, but Marcus and the girl are the only ones they'll recognize. They will need to be hidden. You can use the cart for them to hide in and have the boys pull it."

"The urban guards are not stupid," Marcus retorted. "They will be searching anyone and everyone, and two boys pulling a vegetable cart will be enough to warrant a search."

"True," said Festus with a grin. "But this is no vegetable cart." He led them outside and lifted a large piece of sack cloth. Lucilla stifled a scream with her hand. Staring back at them from the cart were five dead bodies.

"The best way for you to get out alive," said Festus, "is to pretend to be dead."

"I can't...I can't lie on them!" Lucilla whispered.

"You won't lie on them," replied Festus with a wicked grin. "You'll need to lie under them."

Despite Lucilla's protests, Marcus and the boys knew that Festus was right. A cartload of dead bodies destined for a public grave was less likely to invite unwelcome interest from the guards than anything else. They lifted the bodies aside to make space for Marcus, then coaxed Lucilla to get in next. She buried her face in her hands before they placed a second layer of sacking on top of them, followed by the bodies.

"One more thing," said Festus. "My boys are positioned along the route to the river. As we pass them, they will follow. When we get to the boat, we'll be there to distract any guards who might take an interest."

"You've done well, boy," came Marcus's muffled voice. "I'm sure you kept some of the money I gave you for the boatman?"

"Of course!" Festus grinned, and they heard Marcus chuckle.

"Festus," Arthur added. "Thanks. I thought you would turn us in."

"If it was just you, I would have. But him?" Festus nodded at the cart, then began to stroll away. "He was already a hero on these streets. Now he's killed one of the most hated men in Rome, and most people will thank him for it.

Follow after me, but keep your distance so I can warn you of any trouble."

Arthur and Finn got into position at the front of the cart, lifted the yoke, and began to pull. The cart was heavy and it took a big heave to get it going. Once the wheels were rolling, the boys were able to keep pace with Festus easily enough. Festus kept to the alleys for as long as possible, but eventually he led them onto a larger and much busier road.

"What do we say if we're stopped?" said Arthur suddenly. "We don't know where we're supposed to be heading!"

"Stop a moment!" someone whispered behind them and the boys froze, the cart knocking into them from behind. Then Finn realized the voice had come from inside the cart.

"Esquiline Hill. That's where the mass funerals happen." There was something very creepy about hearing those words come from a cartload of corpses. Finn shivered, grateful all of a sudden that he was pulling the cart, and not in it. Looking back, Finn recognized some of Festus's gang strolling along behind them. The boys resumed their progress with another heave, and soon noticed that they were heading slightly downhill. Ahead of Festus, the boys could see the black scar of the river for the first time.

Suddenly, the incline steepened and gravity began to drag the cart downhill. The boys found that they needed to pull back on the yoke rather than push against it. Finn's foot slipped in the mud. He stumbled backward, throwing Arthur off balance. The cart quickened and the boys scrambled back into position, knowing that if it ran away from them, Lucilla and Marcus would almost certainly be discovered. As they struggled to regain control, Arthur glanced ahead and swore.

"Guards! Festus is talking to a bunch of guards. What's he doing?"

"Calm down," his brother urged. "If he wanted to turn us in, he would have done it already. He must be trying to distract them. Just keep walking past them." As they drew nearer, one of the guards turned and stared at them, then came up to them as the cart drew up to guards. Finn and Arthur stared intently at the road in front of them, and carried on until Finn could not help glancing

around. The soldier was walking along beside the cart with one hand on the sack cloth. He lifted it up and Finn held his breath, waiting for the inevitable shout.

But the soldier merely wrinkled his nose and dropped the cloth, turning back to the other guards. Moments later, Festus reappeared in front and led them on. The brothers glanced at one another, wide-eyed, too tense to notice the stench of sewage that drifted toward them as they approached the river. Just as the road was about to lead them onto a bridge, Festus turned and headed along a lane that followed the riverbank. He stopped at the top of a flight of steps. A small boat was moored at the bottom.

Finn and Arthur set the cart down, bursting with excitement now, the promise of escape was so near. Festus, saying nothing, made his way to the back of the cart.

Behind them came a shout. "You there! Stay where you are!"

Finn turned. "Oh no," he breathed. Arthur spun around. The blood drained from his face, as he discovered what Finn was looking at.

Back at the junction with the main road were two of the guards Festus had spoken to.

And they were running their way.

CHAPTER 10

Finn and Arthur froze. Festus put his fingers to his lips, whistled loudly, then turned and bolted along the riverside. The guards ran toward them, swords drawn and raised. In the boat, a black-cloaked boatman emerged and began untying his moorings frantically.

"Marcus," Arthur whispered. "Guards! Jump out on my call."

Up on the bridge a great commotion broke out, and for a moment, the boys thought that more people were coming for them. Then some of the wooden stalls on the bridge went up in flames. In the sudden light, Festus's gang could be seen dancing around, pushing and shoving everyone within reach.

"He's creating a decoy!" said Finn, breathlessly as the guards approached.

"You, boys," one of them barked. "Take two steps away from the cart. Run, and you will die." Arthur and Finn did as they were told. The guards rushed to the back of the cart and tore off the cover. In seconds, they had dragged the five dead bodies onto the ground and exposed the final covering.

"Now!" yelled Arthur, pulling back his own

cloak and reaching for the short sword that Marcus had given him earlier. Finn did the same, just as Marcus leaped up to a crouch in the cart.

"You are outnumbered," Finn shouted at the guards. But Marcus was in no mood to negotiate. He leaped down from the cart with a wild cry, punching the hilt of his sword into one guard and knocking him into the other so they both collapsed to the ground. Two quick thrusts followed, and moments later, Marcus was dragging their bodies down the steps. He flung them in the river in front of the terrified boatman.

"Time to earn your money, old man," said Marcus, and he beckoned the boys to come down. Finn helped Lucilla out of the cart, and all four of them made their way down to the boat. They scrambled swiftly to the bow and laid down on their backs so they could not be seen from land. The boatman said nothing. He pushed away from the bank with a long pole, and steered them out toward the middle of the river. The current began to take them slowly away from the bridge.

None of them could have said how long they lay like that, silently waiting for the call that would announce the boat was about to be searched by more guards. But the sounds of the city gradually diminished, until all they could hear was the blowing of the wind, the lapping of the water, and the steady wooden thud of the boatman's pole against the side of the boat.

The moon shone through wispy clouds, casting just enough faint light to illuminate Marcus's face staring up at the sky. When Finn turned to look at the gladiator, something burned in the man's eyes.

"You're a free man," said Finn.

"Yes," said Marcus, glancing over at Lucilla, who had fallen into a fitful sleep. "And now, at last, I have something to protect again."

The moon disappeared again, as the boat entered a thick river mist. They were plunged into total darkness. As he felt the spinning sensation that signaled the end of another adventure, Finn reached out to hold Arthur's arm. Relief poured over them as the familiar shapes of the furniture in the Professor's study began to materialize out of the darkness...

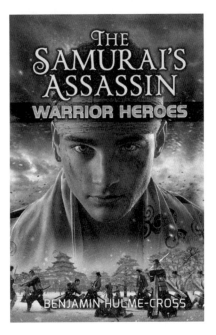

WARRIOR HEROES
The Samurai's Assassin

Benjamin Hulme-Cross

Trapped in their great-grandfather's museum
and visited by the restless ghosts of warriors past,
Arthur and Finn must travel back in time and
rewrite history to set the ghosts free. Will the boys
be able to stop the powerful warlord Kenji Kuroda
from seizing power once and for all?

Extract from
WARRIOR HEROES
The Samurai's Assassin

Finn drifted lazily toward consciousness, dreaming that he was leaping to impossible heights, then rushing back down to Earth, only to leap even higher into the air once more. He licked his lips and tasted brine, noting that heavy rain was pelting his back as he took another giant leap skyward. It was just as he reached the highest point of the arc and hung there for a moment, waiting for the fall, that he woke with a jolt.

A huge wave rolled forward and Finn swooped down the back of it, slipping off the plank of wood that he had been half lying on. He gulped down a mouthful of seawater as he shouted out in panic. Spluttering, he kicked, hoisting himself back onto the tiny float. He blinked, trying to shake the water out of his eyes before the next wave began to lift him up again.

As he reached the top of the wave, he twisted around, praying he would see some way out of this nightmare that he had swapped for the Professor's study. He felt slightly better when he saw that the waves were surging toward land, and that he was in the middle of a small bay.

Finn pulled himself farther forward on the plank, as though he were lying on a surfboard. As he rose with the next wave, he pushed himself up on his arms to get a better view. He could see very little of the shoreline through the torrent of rain, but what he did see turned his stomach. The feeling of relief he had felt just moments before quickly evaporated. Ahead of him, the huge waves were breaking over a line of jagged rocks that stuck up out of the sea like teeth. And he was heading straight for them.

About the author

Growing up in London I spent a lot of time sitting on the Underground, daydreaming and reading books. Historical adventures in far-flung lands were always my favorite, and I used to love visiting castles and ruins.

After I left home, I lived in Japan for a while and learned all about the Samurai. Now I've swapped the city for the countryside, and as well as reading books I also write stories and plays for young people.

The thing I like most about being a writer is playing around with ideas for stories in my head—which is daydreaming really, so not much has changed!